Love in the last days

Martyn Becker

Published by Martyn Becker, 2024.

LOVE IN THE LAST DAYS

First edition. August 11, 2024.

ISBN: 979-8227625939

Written by Martyn Becker.

Table of Contents

In the light of the moon

It's a cold winters Friday night again, and as he has grown accustom to, Michael is alone in front of his TV, looking for something interesting to watch, something to distract him from the fact that its weekend again, and he is alone. Scrolling through social media seems equal these days as reading spam emails and he already knows that there are only attention seeking woman on Tinder. Looking at world events, every city seems to be Babylon, every government ancient Rome, once amazing places turned to Sodom, people have grown loveless, without compassion, ignorant to truth and easily deceived, so much information and yet so uninformed, distracted by media and occupied with entertainment, freedom is an illusion and all seems to lead to chaos and destruction. Indoctrination has spread from television, to social media, universities and even schools. Is it possible to find love in a loveless world, to have a love story for the ages, written in the last days? How can you find a lasting love, when everyone only acts on lust and instant gratification? People living for self, godless and without compassion.

He can go out and meet a nice girl, hook up for the evening or even find someone to date for a couple of weeks, just not to be lonely, but what's the point, he has done this before, and besides he is looking for something real, something lasting and true, that one thing that seems to be just out of reach, true love, that once in a life time, his own love story. But what he is longing for in his heart, his mind has already decided does not exist anymore. That type of love is only in the movies or a few lucky ones from the previous generation, like his parents, looking over to a picture of them from their engagement party back in the good old 1960s. They met by chance, He was from Johannesburg, South Africa, and she was from Atlanta and she joined her best friend for a weekend away in New York, who was visiting her sister. So they went to a house party, and there was the man she would marry only six months later. You know how it goes, its love at first sight, the chemistry was just right and they both just knew, blah blah blah! They were happily married with life's ups and downs for 50 years, they truly did the 'till death do us part' as they promised in their vows.

So, how did Michael end up here, alone on a Friday night, 80s rock music in the background, holding a picture of his parents, dreaming about something he doesn't know, being a total girl about it? If his best friend Jason ever knew he was such a romantic at heart and that his favourite genre is romantic comedies, he would never hear the end about it.

Born and raised in the big apple, life was pretty awesome for the kid raised in the 90s from Brooklyn, he had the nuclear family, the friends and living the American dream, growing up as a kid. He got his marketing degree from University and did all the things you'd expect a teenager and student to do. Real upstanding guy, a gentleman with the whole old school approach to life, values, integrity, passion and heart. He is the life of the party, an extrovert, the friend you can count on, the guy you want on your team, tall, dark hair with some silver in between, athletic build, broad shoulders, a strong chiselled jawline and a smile that can make the most confident girls blush, yet he is down to earth and sometimes even a bit shy.

He has been through life as we all have, had success and failures, lessons learned, character built, dues paid, things not always working out, but somehow still seems to manage. Sure, he is not where he wants to be or needs to be in life, and actually life has been better than it seems to be now. The world has changed, people, dating, technology, cost of living and the list goes on, but Michael has stood by his values and old school soul. He is living life his way and not giving in to all this political correct, greater good, socially acceptable nonsense that's been taking place. He went from a big group of friends, party every night, sports bars and sporting events, slowly to the remaining one best friend, Jason that he has known since high school, going out for a beer or catching a game on TV while having a barbeque.

He recently got laid off by his company as the recession continues, his parents both passed away in the last 18 months, his social life collapsed and he hasn't had a girlfriend since the pandemic days. Freelancing on several jobs from home, pays the bills, even though barely just so. Things have taken an unexpected down turn and he finds himself on the opposite side of where he imagined he would be at this stage of life. He is in a place where he realises, that everything he pursued, with all his abilities and hard work has come to nothing.

His best friend Jason, who has always been a bit of a party animal, couldn't hold down a job, a player, the charming guy who gets the ladies, always out with someone else, never having a relationship, ended up getting married to a girl who's his complete opposite, and he has job security, while Michael, is still single, unemployed, and this at 40! Jason fell for a girl, unexpectedly who tamed him in a way, who turned his lust to love and his passion to purpose, he has proved himself to be a great husband, who knew?

Michael, now having a coffee and vaping on his small balcony. It's been a month since his last cigarette, and the vaping and Nicorette's seems to be a new addiction he has traded up for. Looking over the city, he thinks back to the few girls he's loved, there's been the first love, high school sweetheart Kelly, the blue eyed blonde who ended up breaking his heart, guess that's what you get if you go for the appearance and the girl that everybody wants and that a lot of them got! Then there was Zoey, the one who's heart got you, but her insecurities lost you, Natasha the girl from work, that was a lot of fun, but the bill was due after the fun was had. Even the 'friends with benefits' Christine ended up being so complicated that the benefits ran out and the friendship was lost. There were several girls who had potential, but ended up never being more than just a fling or a night out. Now, Mike is not the type of guy who sleeps around, being a man of passion and intimacy, he tends to drive the girls up the wall, and because he is the way he is, girls fall in love with him quite easily. But he just wants to meet that one, the one he falls in love with, the one who gets him and can see his worth, beyond his charm and physical appearance, a girl who is more into him, than into materialistic things, who he is and not what he can buy for her. Like his last girlfriend Jessica, she wanted a man with ambition, while Michael is a guy who rather wants to be significant than successful.

He thinks back, to all the what if's, if he chose different, if he didn't take her back, if he rather could have met that one girl, or got to know that other one he met, or if he only had the guts that one time, with that girl who just had that something different, special kind of vibe. After this, he wonders if there is really reason left to dream, to hope, that there can still be a meaningful relationship that can make all these wasted years, loneliness, heartbreak and bad choices, worthwhile? After all, you want to share your life with someone, not your memories, you still want things to look forward to, not back on, what about starting a family, or has he missed out on what could have, should have been?

He can't even watch his romantic comedies anymore, it used to be a hope, living through the characters and missing someone he doesn't know, feel good type of emotion, now just sadness and anger, while love songs, he avoids that completely. He acts all tough, like he is completely fine, the whole 'I don't need a woman' and who has time for all that drama, I'm happy just focusing on me, and doing me lies, that he thinks people believe, trying to convince himself. But truth of it is, He is missing her with all his heart, every single day, as if he senses her love like a memory without ever having the experience. His mind is in denial, but his heart has loved her for years, awaiting her arrival to become whole and have a reason for beating again. 'How can you miss someone so much, someone you've never even met?' He thinks frustratingly.

Trying to distract himself he goes on YouTube for some entertainment, when he stumbles upon a video of this beautiful woman with wavy long brown hair, strong green brownish eyes with a sparkle, high cheek bones, and a smile that would make your heart melt. On her channel she's talking about God with such passion, that he can't stop watching, and for the first time he sees someone with that something that he hasn't seen in a woman before, that spirit, soul and being, all that beyond the personality, heart and physical appearance things. Connecting and agreeing with all she is saying, as if she is one spirit with him, He starts to hope again, because for the first time he sees someone who stirs something inside him, deep inside his being, then he realises, this is exactly the type of wife, the type of person I have been looking for, all my life, she is gorgeous, has the personality, heart, soul, spirit and truth, seeing the beauty of God in the soul of a woman, a simple video on his cell phone, restoring his hope of the possibility that there is someone out there like this. Then reality sinks in again, realising although someone like this exists, He is still alone on a Friday night, 40, finding hope in a girl he hasn't even met, or in all likely hood never will. He makes a conscience decision, talking to God, surrendering his desire, his dreams, for God is his hope, regardless of what he desires, his biggest desire is to be a man according to Gods heart, a game changer, a life of purpose, to live for the bigger picture, keeping eyes on eternity, as he decides to let go and let God, no more one foot in the world and one in the kingdom, no more living for self but living for God. Whatever the price, the sacrifice, to live is Christ and to die is gain. He prays that the Holy Spirit will become his thoughts, his words, his ears, his hands and his feet. He does ask God that if it be His will, that he would meet the one that God wants for him, to prepare him to be the man she deserves, and if she is somewhere out there under the same moon, to look up this night and know that God has also answered her prayers and that she may be filled with peace, joy and a new hope. But as for me, he prays I will seek you my Lord, your will, it is no more me who lives for myself, but you who live in me, for your glory, I surrender!

It's the same moment in Miami, and winter seems to have no effect on the sunshine state. A 32 year old Bianca has just returned from a night out with her BFF and sister Jackie. It's the first time the two have had a girl's night out since summer. Bianca just broke up with her boyfriend of 4 months, after she caught him cheating on her. She is so tired of guys, always pretending to be someone they are not, trying to get with the girl that looks to be a challenge. Tired of these fake guys, these man-Childs and lustful boys, trying to get her into bed, calling her a tease and a waste of time if she doesn't 'put out' not seeing any worth past her body, she wants a soulmate, a husband, someone that makes her feel safe, a place that she belongs, that feels like home.' Over the years, she has had repeated disappointments and heartbreak, Jeffrey was her first love and they grew apart, Matt was attractive, but ended up being a cheater, Chris was a smooth talker, a flirt, but again a womanizer, and she made a terrible mistake out of pain and anger by having a one night stand vengeance rebound that just made everything worse, then Richard, he was a dream come true, turned nightmare, emotional and physical abuse, the guy who broke her and led to her losing herself and ended up hating men for more than a year, the last boyfriend, she dated, just not to be alone, so she went into it for the wrong reasons, excluding the countless idiots trying their luck, and others pretending to be friends, with ulterior motives. She has lost her faith in true love, yet she still has a little hope of meeting the right guy, still dreaming of a soulmate, her once in a lifetime. Divided within herself of what she desires and what she have experienced.

Bianca is a cute, petite and sweet girl, a small town type of girl living in the city, she is soft and gentle, an introvert that cares deeply for the people in her life, easy approachable, but not as responsive to flirtation as she used to be, she knows who she is, what she has to offer and what she wants. Loneliness, desperation, charming and attractive guys might have been a weakness in the past, but after all the painful lessons, she finally decides that she won't settle for less than she deserves, she will take her time to get to know a guy well, before dating, that she doesn't need a guy, she wants the right guy, and till then, she will live out herself in other aspects of her life. She has decided that she is done with chasing happiness in all its forms but will rather pursue God and start looking to Him only and not all the things of this life.

Jackie on the other hand has a different approach, she dates a guy for a week or two, maybe even up to a couple months, or one night if he is really hot. She used to be like Bianca, looking for love, and maybe she was expecting it to happen too easily, moved to quickly, as she would go from relationship to relationship, falling in and out of love in weeks, till eventually she just decided to go with the flow, and whatever has the least amount of drama or commitment. As they say goodnight, Bianca again as she always does, tries to convince Jackie to join her for church on Sunday, and as always, Jackie replies sarcastically 'God can find me at work, if He has something to say, he has my email'

Jackie is an atheist and Bianca a Born again Christian, Jackie became an atheist due to several events in her life, her parents' divorce, father who passed away, all the heartbreak and from looking at all the pain in the world, thinking that Christianity is boring and takes all the fun out of life, while Bianca became a born again Christian because of these things, she finds purpose and joy, happiness and peace in her faith. Strange how the same events caused two sisters, so alike to follow different paths, one turning to, and one turning from God. Bianca works as a Media Planner and has been a copywriter, an event coordinator, and has experience in Human resources, Jackie is in sales, and one of the best sales people you'll ever meet. They both grew up in Tampa, before moving with their mom to Miami after the divorce. Bianca was 16, and Jackie 13 at the time. Jackie hated her dad and never had a good relationship with him since, while Bianca reconciled with her dad after high school. She started working straight out of High school, and had different jobs as she tried to find her place in the world. Her active social life also took a big hit when she became a Christian, and made some lifestyle changes. She is no stranger to failure or success and sometimes wishes that someone could be there for her, the way she is there for others, as the weight seems a little heavy to carry on some days.

As they say goodnight, Bianca walks up the steps, she stops, looks up at the moon, takes a deep sigh of relief and cracks a small hopeful smile, and the frustration over men, relationships and the breakup is just lifted in an instant, and she is filled with peace and joy. Getting into bed, she prays the same thing that she has done for years, 'God, please reveal yourself to my sister, let she find her true identity and purpose in you, through your Spirit, I trust you for the right man in my life as per your will and timing, a man who has strong values, old school, a gentleman, a romantic, who wants family, a game changer for your kingdom, I will focus on you, amen'

She opens a new journal and writes down -It is only when we realise that our efforts, our desires and the living for self has only resulted in pain, failure and loss, that we need a saviour, that we need to surrender, to submit to Gods will in faith that we will find peace, freedom and discover what God has instore for us. 'If you hold on to your life, you will lose it, but if you lose it for Jesus, you will find it' 'Seek therefore the kingdom of God first, and all these things will be given to you' and Gods ways are so much higher than our ways'

Changing Seasons

Over the last three weeks, Michaels circumstances has gotten worse, he has been evicted from his apartment and now has a room over at his sisters place, Alicia who is now helping him get by. She is married to Logan for ten years and has an eight year old son named David, and Michael knows he has to make a plan and get back on his feet ASAP. At least he has stopped vaping, more due to circumstance than free will, but he'll take the win!

His confidence has taken a big nose dive, but his faith has leaped forward, for in his darkest moment, he realised that he is nothing without God, and that only God would be able to save him from his fate. Michael has been a strong Christian for years, but slowly moved away from God and towards the world, ambition, success and good times. With all that's been going on, maybe God allowed him his free will, to show him the results of his own effort and pursuits, so that he can learn from it and return to the true source of life and his purpose. He truly believes that all things can work towards good, and that God can do more with what is left, than was has been wasted. He kind of feels like Job, the guy who lost everything, and is looking at this season of his life as a time God is preparing him, for what he has been prepared for, a time of shaping and a time of transition.

Michael has spent all his free time praying, studying the bible again, and completed his book on Identity and purpose, that he felt inspired to finish, since he started on the manuscript more than 4 years ago. Available online, he also sent copies to all his friends. He decided that instead of focusing on his problems, circumstances and everything he cannot do or do not have, he is going to focus on God, what he still has and what he can do, with what he has and where he is, and all he has in Him, seeking first the kingdom of God as he had learned years before, and only now learned how to apply it. He doesn't do the whole church thing, as he sees a big difference between church people and Christian people. He rather focusses on God in a personal relationship than joining the fake, pretend religious gatherings with entertainment rather than worship, and preachers who are more motivational speakers than truth seekers, as he has come to know them. The type of people who will always say that they will pray for you, rather than actually helping you. He realises that he is in a wilderness season and that he is in transition into a new season. A season he cannot see, yet is excited about, going all in for God and letting go of his worldly desires that seem to provide only temporary joy and end in failure or craving more, like a drug, never being satisfied. Yet now in his pursuit of God, he has a new peace, joy and a level of being content.

Following all that has been happening in the world, he can't help but feel that time for humanity is coming to an end, it's exactly as it has been written in the bible how people would be and the things that will take place in the last days. Wars, and rumours of wars, like the war between Israel and Iran, that was over within 6 days, the war in Ukraine that ended up being more complicated than was reported on the news, the invasion of Taiwan by China, earthquakes in various places like the devastating and record breaking earthquake that left Los Angeles and San Francisco with tens of thousands dead, known as the biggest tragedy in American history, the behaviour of people, the moral decline and the move towards what seems to be a centralized global government, the prosecution and censorship of Christians.

While catching the playoffs game between the Knicks and the Heat, at TGI Fridays, Jason tells Michael that he is wasting time on religious nonsense, and the most important thing to do now, is to get a job, any job and worry about himself and not the issues of the world, get back into dating, enjoy the game, even though your team is losing! His wife Nicole agrees, adding that he needs to get laid, he isn't getting any younger. Doing the whole 'friends first' sounds sweet, but it's not realistic, woman want a relationship, not friendship with a possibility, but a commitment. He stands in faith that God will provide and open doors, he will keep his focus on God, Jason then sets him up with the waitress, and He consents and takes her out on a date. The attraction is there, but he finds her to be annoying, without personality and a bit superficial, while he can't stop talking about God. His passion he speaks with and his respectful manner, has captured her attention, and by the end of the night she became saved. On the way home, Michael has tears of joy, thanking God for the best date he has ever been on. An evening that didn't lead to sin, but to salvation.

Meanwhile, Bianca is working hard as a Media Planner at a small Marketing agency, focusing on God and herself and ensuring that she uploads her Christian inspirational videos every single week, hoping it reaches people and brings restoration and repentance. She really finds strength and support from her church friends and she is interested in doing missionary work abroad, not just as a calling, a purpose, but also as a reason to just get away from it all, to experience something else and maybe discover something new in life, she feels stuck, almost like she is moving in circles and not moving forward, the state of her nation, the moral decay, economic collapse, the great California quake, another election result in question, and a leader more concerned on protecting those in power, than helping average Americans, a government not for the people, or by the people, but against the people, a nation divided as if conquered from within. Americans has grown ignorant of God's word and live according to their own pleasures and desperation, tolerating everything that is wrong and avoiding all that is right, maybe people from other countries are still open minded and not as easily influenced by government, media and entertainment. Not even to mention the second so-called pandemic that anyone with half a brain, knows was planned to gain more control and commit mass genocide on the public.

Although she just got out of a relationship, she agrees to go on a date with a guy from church. She is open to possibilities of friendship that might develop into something more. They go for bowling and a bite to eat, and she sees straight through this guy, another pretender, a smooth talker who wants one thing only, trying to impress her with his success. She politely and firmly lets him down easy and takes an Uber back home. Just more confirmation for her to keep her focus on Jesus and not get distracted with anything else.

While staying with his sister, Michael's faith has grown stronger as he is inspired by his sister and brother in law, he has published his book and hope that it reaches people and brings change and restoration to whoever reads it. He also assists his brother in law with marketing for his business and has found a new joy in the time he spends with his nephew, giving him an excuse to act like a kid again. He has also decided to look for opportunities outside of his comfort zone and even got in touch with his cousin from Cape Town, a beautiful place he visited a couple of years ago.

The evening he joins Jason and Nicole for a barbeque, and amongst the acquaintances is Nicole's friend and his ex-girlfriend Zoey. Whereas Michael's life has gone downhill, Zoey has had nothing but prosperity. Happy for her, he is also annoyed and embarrassed for himself. It is so difficult to remain faithful in God and hopeful of life, when everything keeps going against you and everyone looks at you with pity or judgement, while life has been great to them. Knowing you can't even take someone out for coffee, while those around you are buying new cars, property and flying across the country. After weeks of building hope and confidence, tonight was a real punch in the gut as he heads home and goes straight to bed, just wanting the day to be over.

Over in Miami, its Jackie's birthday party and Bianca is feeling completely out of place. They move in different circles and Jackie's friends are all about the good times, drinking, drugs, parties, one night stands, selfies and celebrities. Again she finds herself irritated at the lustful, shallow guys without any personality trying all the lines on her she has heard before. Has she become old before her time, is she a bit of a prude? No, for her life is more than this, it's deeper and meaningful. When they decide to go out clubbing at midnight, Bianca seizes the opportunity to leave, goes home and straight to bed, much to the disappointment of her sister. She receives a message on her phone from an old friend she hasn't spoken to in months, reading 'you have grown too big for this place, you are to be replanted to bear much fruit, and you are to go to the land that has been prepared for you. Just wanted to share, was on my heart.'

The next day, Bianca has a meeting with an organization called One Way, they do various outreach and missionary programs around the world, and she signs up for a year's outreach in Cape Town, taking the leap of faith and following her gut, while also thinking how crazy this is, to make such a big move, a decision to leave everything she knows, for all that's unseen and unknown. She is usually someone who makes informed decisions and take calculated risks, but she is trying to make more choices out of faith and obedience.

On sharing the news with her sister, who is still nursing a hangover, Jackie applauds her decision, thinking that it would be a great adventure for her, and that for once she stepped outside her comfort zone, did something impulsive without overthinking as she usually does. Once she has received a sponsor she would have 30 days, before leaving.

Michael has just received great news! He was made an offer at a company in Cape Town as Marketing Manager after his cousin shared his resume with his contacts and they did a remote interview with him. He thought long and hard about it, prayed about it and after a couple of days got the confirmation he needed, and decided to take the job. He loves to be impulsive and allow life to happen, but this is a big life changing decision.

Looking for some fun in the sun, Jason, Nicole, Michael and friends decides to go down to Miami for couple of days. On arriving in Miami, Nicole and Kate meets up with her old friend from college, Jackie and her sister Bianca for a girls night out on Ocean drive, while Michael, Jason and Brad is having a boys night out, catching the playoffs game between the Heat and the Hawks.

Meeting up later in the evening, Nicole tells Michael that she has met the ideal girl for him, and that she wants to introduce to him the following night. After showing him her picture, he couldn't believe his eyes, as this was the same girl from the YouTube videos he has been following. He hesitantly agrees, as he really would like to meet her, but already knows he is leaving the country soon, and thinks that irony has a weird sense of humour, to put him in such a situation. Thinking maybe God is testing him or the enemy is tempting him. He then breaks the news to his friends, that he accepted an opportunity in Cape Town and will be leaving in a couple of weeks, and he just needs to organise the needed finances to settle his debt and cover himself for the trip. Nicole thinks that as soon as he meets Bianca, he will have a change of heart.

So the following night they all go out together, all except for Bianca. Jackie admitting that her sister is not one to go out two nights in a row and not looking to meet anyone at this stage, while she also needed to do her weekly video. After a night out of enjoying the neon lights and palm trees of South beach, Jackie texts her sister mockingly on what an amazing night she missed out on, and an amazing guy she could have met.

The next afternoon as the sun is setting over the Atlantic Ocean, Jason and Nicole has date night, Michael is sitting on Miami Beach wearing board shorts and his vintage Bon Jovi t-shirt, again experiencing a moment of missing that someone next to him, thinking how this could be his last day on a beach in Florida, a place that he has made many memories over the years while, only one life guard tower over, sits a lonely Bianca, a slight breeze blowing through her beautifully styled long brown hair, experiencing the same emotion, while listening to some classic 80s love songs on her iPod. She looks over the ocean, realising that one of these days, she would be on the opposite side of the Atlantic. She stands up and decides to go for a walk down the beach, and so also does Michael. While walking, Bianca turns around, realising she has a meeting with One Way, and seconds later Michael passes the spot she was just sitting a moment ago.

The last day in Miami, a well-known Christian artist is performing at Bianca's church, so you know she's up for worship with one of her favourite artists, while only four rows back, stands Michael, also a big fan, who decided to attend while he is down here in Miami, connecting to God through worship. Half way through he notices this woman, four rows ahead of him, completely immersed in worship, thinking to himself how awesome and real, raw and honest a moment this woman is experiencing and that he would love to have a woman like that beside him, without even seeing her face, just her long beautiful brown hair and petite built, with skinny jeans, off the shoulder top and sneakers. The moment passes and a few songs later he also finds himself immersed in song, Bianca looking over her shoulder at her friends behind her, suddenly notices a guy four rows back, tall, dark and handsome, with his hands stretched out, worshiping with a tear rolling down his cheek, thinking to herself 'that is exactly what she wants'.

Afterwards he gets into a taxi to go back to the hotel and upon leaving he recognises the girl who was, moments ago only four rows ahead, seeing her face, he realises that this was Bianca, and for a brief moment she looks up and sees him as they smile simultaneously at each other.

Driving back home to Atlanta, Michael thinks of how this is just another should have, could have been situation, wondering what if?

Bianca, starts doubting her decision to go to South Africa, what if she goes on this trip and because of it, doesn't meet the man of her dreams, someone like that guy she saw earlier today. It's with a heavy heart she goes to bed and pray, saying that she would sacrifice love and what she so desired, for Gods will and not her will as she wipes a tear from her cheek, knowing what she has to do is greater than what she wants to have, asking God as always to reveal Himself to her sister, she doesn't want to leave her, while she is so far away from God, but His will and not hers, she will let go and let God.

Two weeks later, Michael receives a notification of a payment, made to his account from the platform where he has self-published his book, just a month earlier, he is completely overwhelmed, as the amount paid to his account from eBook sales is enough to cover his debt, his flights and cover him for a couple of months in Cape Town. There was even enough, that he decided to give some back to God, through a sponsorship for missionaries to South Africa, from a flyer he had kept from the worship service he attended in Miami. Sharing this wonderful news with his sister and friends, as he starts to prepare for his trip.

At that very moment, Jackie calls her sister, sobbing and barely able to get any words out, Bianca rushes over to her apartment. On arriving at her place, Jackie runs and hugs her sister in tears, apologising repeatedly. Once she finds her composure she reveals to Bianca that her college friend, Nicole, sent her an eBook about Identity and purpose, to her work email, and decided to read the book as it was sent by her friend and written by the guy she met recently on a night out, while reading the book and not being able to stop, it touched her soul, she finally understood, everything aligned, she gave her life to Jesus. Every wall she has built was broken down, all her pain was gone, the hate, the questions, bitterness, in a moment everything made sense, and all that mattered was the one who matters, Jesus. She cried like she never cried before, not from pain, but from release, from His love and from being overwhelmed by His grace. Bianca smiling with tears in her eyes tells Jackie about her famous words, 'if God has something to say, he can find me at work, he has my email' as they both laugh and cry, hugging and pray together for the first time, ever. She again realises the faithfulness and goodness of God, her prayers for her sister has finally been answered, God saved her, not through her direct influence, but through her prayers, an old friend and a book from a stranger, through her unbelief he made her a believer and now Bianca can go to Africa, without the concern for her sister.

Even more good news and answered prayer happened the next morning, when Bianca received a call from One-Way, that her entire missionary trip to Cape Town has been paid in full by an anonymous sponsor and that she needs to prepare to leave in a month.

Bianca makes an entry in her journal -The seasons of winter through spring has been an uncertain time of transition and change, of letting go of everything that was, everything familiar, and though things are unclear, it seems that as life has fallen apart, it has actually fallen into place. Letting go of what was, and preparing for what is to come! Moving in faith to the purposes of God.

Cape of Good Hope

As the summer starts, Bianca in Miami, and Michael in Atlanta starts preparing for their new lives in South Africa, with no idea what to expect, and no idea that their lives are set to change forever. All they know is that it's winter in Cape Town and that they are heading to a country with failing infrastructure and a struggling economy, in a lot of ways they are leaving the known luxuries and the familiar for something less and unknown.

After an emotional goodbye to Jackie and her mom, Bianca boards a direct flight to Cape Town, relieved that her sister has become born again and will also move in with her mom, as the two will now support each other, and their relationship has also been healed. Some system issues, results in her flight being delayed by a few hours, On take-off she looks down, seeing the States fade in the background, and with that says goodbye to all her disappointments and heartbreaks, all the tears she cried and also to all the wonderful memories she has made, the friendships she's had and everyone she has ever known, starting a new chapter of her life.

Michael had his own farewell party and the next day gets a connecting flight via New York, goes to one last ball game at Yankee stadium, says goodbye to the empire state and ends up landing around the same time as the flight from Miami. At baggage claim, Michael sees the face of someone he through he would never see in his life again, it's the YouTube girl, the girl from Miami, its Bianca, over at the next baggage carousel! She notices him, looks away and looks up again, recalling his face from the worship night in Miami. Hesitant, nervous and excited, Michael walks over to Bianca, their eyes lock and he greets her with a gentle smile 'Hi' and she responds with a shy smile 'hey'. Chris Tomlin, Miami he points, Bianca from Miami, she replied, with a shy chuckle he takes her hand, its Michael from Atlanta. So they started talking, about where they are from and what they are doing in Cape Town.

She joins him for a coffee, and it is instant attraction, chemistry and something unexplainable, they felt like they have always known each other, like there is this connection, this timeless tie they had, something supernatural. He looked at her like she was the only woman on earth, and she looked at him like he was made just for her. After having a coffee together, spending more time in each other's eyes, blushing, giggling like teenagers on a first date, they both find it refreshing to have an open and honest conversation with someone, who just gets you. They exchange numbers and Michael picks up his rental car. Driving out of the parking lot, he saw Bianca standing in the drop off zone, and it so turns out that her driver had some car trouble, so Michael takes her to the place she will be staying. Neither capable of saying goodbye, they go out for lunch and keep discovering how much they have in common in their values, faith and character, it's like they are two different people with once soul and one heartbeat, the same spirit but different personalities, sure he will tell you she supports the wrong sports teams and she will say that he is a little bit too into rock music. In the ways that they are different, they actually complement each other, and the strength of the one seems to be the weakness of the other.

As the sun sets, they drive up to signal hill, and there outstretched to the one side is the Atlantic Ocean, with Cape Town to the other side, in the shadow of Table Mountain. They share this beautiful sunset in silence, just being in this moment together. It wasn't that long ago they were both, alone on the same beach in Miami looking at the sunset over the other side of the Atlantic, having a void inside themselves, now standing on the opposite side of the Atlantic, together watching a sunset, with that void being replaced with a wholeness, and warmth that cannot be explained, but they both try to deny. Heading down to the Harbour for dinner, before dropping her off at what was a first in so many ways for them both. The uncertainty and being alone in a new country, has suddenly started to feel like home, on the very first day, they found each other and now faces uncertainty, together. Cautiously hopeful, of what this can become.

Amazing how years of misfortune, bad choices, and life, can all change in a single day, a moment in time, and how destiny as it seems, will find you in unexpected ways if you are trusting and following the source of love itself, the author of life, and the one who knows the end from the beginning, when it all seems lost and hopeless, He always has a plan, if we let go and let God.

Both of them take the next few days to settle in, go through orientation in their own way of the new opportunity and challenges they face, while constantly messaging each other, till late at night. Early Saturday morning Michael picks Bianca up at her place, as they head out for the day to explore the greater area outside Cape Town, road tripping around the Cape peninsula. Discovering not just the beauty of this place, but the beauty within each other, their shared passions, when Bianca discovers that the book Michael wrote, was the book that changed her sister's life and he realises that the organization that he donated to, was the same one that brought her here. Learning he was the guy, her sister wanted to set her up with they also discovered that a few years ago, they were both in Savannah, at the same club on the same night. This was the night Bianca made a big mistake, and Michael was a little too much into the party lifestyle. If they had met that night, it would only result in a regret for them both. Just more than a year ago, Michael was the best man at Jason and Nicole's wedding, and his date would have been Jackie, a bridesmaid, and Bianca also a guest, who had to cancel, due to their father passing away. Shocked and amazed, they were overwhelmed by the will and working of God, and how he truly does work all things to work out for the good, to those who seek him, and senses that they were destined to meet now. Desire to jump into whatever this could become, to react to this attraction and chemistry, yet holding back the impulse to do so, both have been hurt too many times, cautiously excited, not trying to show it, while trying to focus on the reason the came here.

After an amazing day of mountain passes, beautiful beaches and the ambience of restaurants they go back to Bianca's and Michael decides to make his speciality pasta dish for them, while she keeps him company, they both enjoy a fine cape wine together. Things keep building up between the two, as they now find themselves more infatuated with each other, the slightest accidental touch causes Bianca to get goose bumps all over, while it takes all his self-control for Michael not to pull her close and kiss her with absolute passion. As the cape winter night gets colder and it starts to rain outside, he starts a fire for them in the fireplace. Sitting next to each other on the couch, drinking wine, as they share more intimate details and personal experiences of their lives, seeing, relating and empathising with each other, laughing, even joke fully mocking each other, they grow closer and closer and the connection is undeniable. The sparkle in Bianca's green brownish eyes seems to hypnotise Michael, while the fire reflecting in his big brown eyes, seems to create a fire in her heart. So in tuned, and lost in each other, without realising, it is now dawn, and they spent the entire night in each other's company. Neither can stop smiling, nor stop talking, but with the sunrise the tiredness starts to settle in. Still drizzling outside, he insists on saying goodbye at the door, and after a long lingering hug, he walks to the car, thinking how badly he wanted to kiss her, Bianca still standing in the door watching him leave, in two minds, with the hope that he turns around and kisses her, and afraid that if he does, she will be at his mercy.

Throughout the following week, they keep messaging each other throughout the day and night, and Bianca looks for any excuse to see him, asking him to fix her kitchen cabinet door, and while he is there to have dinner with her, he does the same, just casually stopping by for coffee as he was in the area, and brought some Krispy crème doughnuts that he knew was her guilty pleasure.

Their interests is not in themselves but in each other and the goodness and mysteries of God. She is completely captivated by his passion for God and gains so much wisdom and insight from him and he in return learns so much about the grace and heart of God from her as their friendship also takes them into a deeper relationship and understanding of God.

The weekend they attend their first rugby match together with Bianca's friends from One Way, Neil and Jenni. They are originally from South Dakota, and have been leading the organisation in Cape Town for the last five years. They have been happily married for ten years and have two kids, an 8 year old boy named Brett and a 6 year old girl named Chelsea. Michael it seems has found a new sport he can follow and a new friend to enjoy it with. Afterwards they join the couple for a braai at their place. A Braai is like a barbeque on a next level. During the evening Neil and Jenni can't stop talking about what a cute couple Michael and Bianca would make, saying that the attraction and chemistry is very obvious, leaving the two blushing.

The next day they go to an outreach together, to serve children at an orphanage. Michael is surprised at how much he enjoys the day, spending time with the kids, feeling as if they have blessed him more than he has them, and Bianca is impressed with how much the kids loves Michael and how patient and good he is with them. So much so that Jenni caught Bianca completely distracted and staring at him.

The desire they have for each other is written all over their faces and the longing all over their actions, she is captivated by him and he is hypnotised by her.

Another week of late night conversations, walking on the beach, dinner with friends and introducing Bianca to his cousin Steven. After meeting her, Steven suggests to Michael that he should really do something about Bianca, he would have, but she is clearly crazy over Mike as he is over her. They have grown so close, they have established a good friendship over the last month, and he doesn't want to lose that, but he wants so much more, the desire to kiss her and to be with her has been building up and building up, that he feels so nervous to kiss her, like he did the first time he kissed a girl, as if he needs to create the perfect moment for the perfect kiss. She is more than what he wants, and he feels that she deserves more than what he has to offer.

Bianca on a video call with Jackie, admits for the first time, that she is in love. And it's in love like never before, on a deeper level, more intense. He is everything and so much more than what she has dreamed of, and after getting to know him as a friend, she knows that she wants him, but is unsure if he wants her, maybe the attraction, the chemistry, the way he is with her, the way he looks at her, winks and smiles, is all in her head, that she wants to see it? Maybe they need to spend more time together as friends and slowly approach a relationship or maybe it is okay to follow your heart and dive in. Jackie suggests that she goes out on a date with another guy, and that Michael's reaction would answer her doubts, or that she has to turn up the heat and invite him over for dinner with some added romance.

It's Saturday afternoon and the two are sitting on the beach talking about things they have and haven't done, when Michael asks Bianca if she had ever danced with someone on the beach. As she replies no, he grabs her hand and asks her for a dance. They slow dance without music on the beach with her hair waving in the breeze. They are face to face, as she glances at his lips, he bashfully smiles, then he kisses her hand, and keeps holding her hand as they slowly walk down the beach, both with a shy smile on their face. He opens the car door for her as he always does and they go to Bianca's for the evening. She prepares dinner as he starts up the fireplace. After a Candle lit dinner with few words and many smiles they are back on the couch, whispering conversation with the fire crackling in the background. They keep touching each other accidentally on purpose and eventually Bianca gets up to make them coffee. While waiting for the water to boil, standing against the cupboards on opposite sides in silence and in each other's eyes, She bites her lip, he winks at her,

Michael starts walking over to Bianca, his heart racing, she steps forward with bated breath, and finally, after an immense build up, after holding it in, holding it back, she puts her arms around his neck, his arms around her waist and back, pulling her closer, they share a kiss, so passionate, so beautiful, a pure emotion that no words ever spoken or written can express, all condensed in one spectacular kiss, a kiss that heals all hurts, creates a new hope, a kiss that resurrects love. When words fail, and the heart expresses itself through a kiss. A moment that makes time stand still, and ripples throughout the universe. Their eyes meet as their lips part slowly, breathing heavily and feeling faint, he slowly moves away, both speechless, and they smile simultaneously. Blushing with a big smile on her face, she manages to make coffee. Back on the couch they stare, smile and giggle at each other while drinking coffee, that is until they grab each other tight, kissing passionately. As things heat up, they take a breather, before sinking into each other again and again, this continues throughout the rest of the evening, till eventually she falls asleep in his arms, in front of the fireplace.

The next morning she awakens and just enjoys the moment in his arms, he too is awake, just holding her in his arms and soaking up the moment. Eventually they get up, have breakfast and Michael leaves after a half an hour good bye kiss, Bianca closes the door, falls back on the couch, smiling from ear to ear, her eyes lit up like Times square in New York, hands in her hair and her feet kicking in the air of excitement. Michael drives back home in a trance, completely oblivious to his surroundings, he can't stop smiling, filled with excitement and overwhelming joy as the sun rises over the cape, the Cape of Good Hope.

Bianca writes in her journal –is this love, the love I have been searching for? It feels different this time. By focusing on God, has he blessed me with this? After everything, could it be this simple and happen so easily, how can this feel so right, is this my meant to be? If this is from You, my Lord, can I ask for a sign? That he will take my hand and pray over us, and to kiss me on my forehead or to remove him from my life, should he not be sent by you.

Sunsets

Oh, the feeling of being in love, walking around with that stupid smirk on your face all the time, oblivious to what is happening around you, as your thoughts has been taken captive by one person, and your heart has come alive again. Inspired like a poet, dreaming like a child, feeling as though you are walking on water and floating through the air. An intense excitement when they received messages from each other, their hearts sinking when hearing each other's voice, a simple touch causing electricity flowing through your entire body, with your only desire in life, to be together all the time, counting the minutes until you see each other again.

Mike asks Bianca out on an official date, giving her orchids on arrival, a slow passionate kiss and complimenting her on how stunning she looks, as she always does. They go to a romantic restaurant, with an outside gazebo, full of fairy lights and acoustic music in the background. Most of the evening is spent in each other's eyes, few is said, and much is unspoken. Afterward he takes her home, walks her to her door, she invites him in for coffee. He declines and insists on leaving the evening on a high, as he doesn't trust his ability to have self-control if he stays. He takes her hand and starts to pray for her and for them, for Gods guidance and blessing over their developing relationship and kisses her on her forehead as he says goodbye, leaving her speechless, shocked and wanting more. She watches him drive off, frozen for a moment, she goes inside, leans with her back against the door, a tear flows over her cheek as she thanks God for an answered prayer.

The next day while having coffee at Bianca's, the two are silently staring into each other's eyes, and Bianca says to Michael, 'ask me'. He replies, ask you what? Ask me to be your girlfriend she replies. He shyly smiles, gets on his knee beside her and asks her to be his girlfriend. She pauses a bit to tease him, bites her lip, smiles and says 'I would love to be your girlfriend!' She decides to show him what she had written in her journal, regarding a prayer and a forehead kiss, amazed he acknowledges that as he was walking to his car last night, he asked God that if she is still standing there as he leaves, he will know she is for him, if she already went inside he will remain friends. With their eyes watering, smiling ear to ear they embrace each other and thank God for his blessing and his confirmation.

From a romantic day out in the wine lands traveling to various wine estates on a wine tram, a movie night under the stars, to a pick nick in the beautiful botanical gardens of Kirstenbosch, sunsets on Blouberg beach, hiking in the mountains, swimming under a waterfall, having breakfast on Table Mountain, walking hand in hand on the beach, slow dancing on the balcony, to those small moments of a smile, a look, a kiss, falling asleep in each other's arms, praying hand in hand together, making dinner together, cooking classes and the simplicity and beauty of just being together, with no need to say anything, go anywhere or do anything. Happiness is in each other's presence, belonging in each other's eyes and home is being together.

This new found love has inspired new creativity for Michael in his job, and a new level of strength and inspiration for Bianca in her ministry, as it has seemed to not only fuel the two of them in all aspects of life, but enabled them to become more themselves than ever before.

They have started a new relationship and a new season of life, together, developing as individuals, growing closer and deeper together, making new friends together and exploring this beautiful new place they call home. Strange how finding a place you belong, ended up being a person, that all was needed for you to become more you was someone who loves you just for being you. A love penetrating each other's soul. Reaching a connection beyond the natural physical world, beyond human understanding, something that seems to be linked to eternity itself. This is what they experience as they start living in their love story over the following weeks.

Michael has also joined Bianca as a co-host on her YouTube channel that is reaching more people every week, with more than ten thousands subscribers, he has also found a new purpose in assisting Bianca in her missionary work, he is great with kids and a strong influencer for teenagers. They even started their own small group of a home church.

This relationship has brought them closer to God, given them more strength, inspiration, peace and overwhelming joy in life, a sense of belonging and home in each other, as they have found love and beauty in a world of chaos.

Another sunset. Michael and Bianca on the beach, walking hand in hand, as the waves crash and a light breeze fills the air, the sun sets over the Atlantic, Bianca sits between Michaels legs, with her head on his chest, looking back up at him, as he kisses her gently on her forehead.

There are certain things that she absolutely loves about him, the way he smiles and winks at her, his hugs, anything he does with his hands, the way she feels safe in his arms and, his forehead kisses. How passionate he speaks about God, his enthusiasm for life, strength, his cooking, that he is a romantic, a gentleman and an old school guy with a big hart. The way he can easily pick her up with one arm, yet has such a gentle touch, the broad shoulders and the silver grey hair that looks like natural high lights.

He is crazy about everything she is, her long brown wavy hair, her green brownish eyes that stares into his soul, her perfectly shaped and toned body, the way she carries herself, her confidence and humility, the caring and kindness, the look of admiration, the way she smiles and bites her lip, how she runs her finger through his hair, her laugh and her feminine husky voice. Her cooking is alright, but boy can she bake! Her love for God, and how Spirit filled she is. They both learn so much about God from each other, he has a mind for Christ and she has a heart for God.

They have developed their little hobbies and routines, movie night, candle light dinner evenings, load shedding fireplace romance nights, dancing, sunsets on the beach, hiking and pick nicks, working with orphans and the homeless, cuddle and binge watching tv shows, and as often as possible doing something new and discovering new places. From horse riding to kite surfing and sandboarding. Their shared favourite place, is where they had their first moment, signal hill.

After a rugby game at Cape Town Stadium with Neil and Jenni, they join them for a braai. While the two men are barbequing the ladies enjoy a glass of wine on the patio. Jennifer tells Bianca what a perfect couple she and Michael makes, and that people who has seen them together, knows that they have seen true love. Blushing Bianca nods while looking over at the love of her life, knowing he is the one in her heart, while her mind still doubts, thinking it's too good to be true, since it's only been several weeks. He is my world, but we haven't even said that we love each other yet, she responds, as Jenni replies, you don't have to say it, it's written all over you both. Bianca also admits that they haven't been together in that way yet, and it is becoming almost impossible not to, she doesn't want to get married just because she might lose self-control, but she doesn't want to disobey God and mess up the best thing she has ever had. Jenni tells her that it doesn't matter how long you are together, before you get engaged or married. Your heart, your intentions and your commitment is all that matters.

Over at the 'braai' Neil glances back at the ladies and tells Michael how awesome it is that they found each other, asking him if she is the one. He asks how you he knew Jenni was the one. It's something you just know, it's something clear and obvious, it's your soul recognising itself in someone else, it's different from what you are used to, it's deeper than attraction, shared interests and good conversation. It's the realisation that although you are complete as a person, you are half of something bigger, a connection to something supernatural. For the first time he admits that he loves her, and that he knows she is the one, but is fearful of the thought that he somehow finds a way to mess up the best thing that has ever happened to him. She deserves the world, and all I want is to be with her. Neil replies to him 'then you know what to do, no sense in wasting more time, follow your heart and leave the rest to God'

After dinner the two couples discuss the differences of the US and South Africa. After the collapse of the dollar and the stock exchange, the world reserve became the ID, -international digital dollar, issued by the World Bank and backed by gold, oil and other physical assets. OWSE, the one world stock exchange, also consolidated all the stock markets as a global economy was formed, linked to a cashless society, providing more security and easing trade between counties. In South Africa, people are still using the local currency, the Rand, cash and only uses ID for international trade. In the US you have a social credit rating based on your carbon footprint, purchase behaviour, social media activity, and religious affiliation, a higher score gives you access to more freedoms, less tax and more discounts, while a lower score means the opposite, where as in South Africa, the system is live, but inactive, mostly used for universal basic income, and national health insurance, of which the funds have mostly been stolen by government corruption. Digital identification and digital passports has been launched worldwide, yet in SA there are many who still has a passport book and ID cards. There seems to be a level of freedom as a benefit of the inadequate government. Not being tracked on where you go or what you purchase, what you do online, basically means they live off the grid and with freedom.

Moreover, people are more real, kinder, less entitled and harder working than the people from the States, although poverty and unemployment is completely out of control. People are more concerned with acquiring the basics here, as to people in the states who are still obsessed with inequality, climate change, gender and other social issues. Digital microchipping has grown popular in the US as people sacrifice freedom for more security, safety, and access to events, and find it more convenient to have a chip in their hand, to scan for everything they need. In South Africa they can't even keep the power on, as there are rolling black outs, called 'load shedding' scheduled daily. Michael and Bianca has adjusted to this, using it as impulsive romance nights at candle light and seems to see and enjoy the upside of every downside. It still beats the climate lockdowns they have in Canada, shutting down the entire grid, every night, except for essential services.

Jenni and Neil has found it increasingly difficult over the past months to do their missionary work and has even been threatened to be arrested for religious intolerance. Since the Abrahamic faith accord was signed by the Pope, Imam and head Rabbi in Jerusalem, it has been declared that all people has faith in the same god, through different approaches and that tolerance, acceptance, peace and unity must be promoted and any division thereof prosecuted accordingly. The UN has welcomed this and governments complied.

Michael also added that he pays more than double the normal tax on earnings from his book, and that it has also has been removed from some platforms and labelled offensive, divisive and non-inclusive. All this for being a Christian and believing that Jesus is the only way. Nonetheless, the more they censor and ban the book, the more the sales increase. All the proceeds going to support Bianca and the ministry. All these things would seem worrying to most, but the four of them seems unaffected by it, and prospering even more.

Another Sunday and another sunset. As they have almost made a tradition of it, Michael and Bianca heads down to the beach, walking hand in hand, as the waves crash and a light breeze fills the air, the sun sets over the Atlantic, Bianca sits between Michaels legs, with her head on his chest, looking back up at him, as he kisses her gently on her forehead, and whispers I love you, and she responds with I love you. This is only a single moment in time, yet it's carved into eternity. A Single moment that has been a thousand moments in the making.

Sunday night is movie, coffee & cuddle night, and afterwards they have their usual half hour goodbye, followed by twenty minutes goodnight messaging later on. Bianca has her weekly video call with Jackie, giving her the detailed updates of her week and the beautiful moment she and Michael shared a little earlier. Jackie has also been promoted to Regional sales manager and started hanging out with Bianca's church friends, who misses her dearly. She has really become a different person, full of peace and joy and things are really working out well for her. She also reconnected with her best friend from school days, Kevin, whom she has been spending a lot of time with lately. Mike also has his video call to his sister back in the states, saying how much their parents would have loved Bianca, wishing they could have met her, and she jokingly responds not have the wedding before the end of the year.

Monday afternoon, Michael drops off a box at Bianca's place as a surprise and on the way back to work, a car skips the intersection and they collide head on. Minutes later, Bianca busy with admin work, gets a phone call, she answers and it's the hospital. Michael has listed her as his next of kin, and he has been in a car accident and admitted to the hospital. In complete disbelief, shock and denial she franticly runs towards Jenni in tears, asking her to drive her to the hospital. Bianca has not set foot in a hospital since her father passed away, remembering all that was left unsaid, she keeps praying in the car all the way to the hospital, hoping for the best and expecting the worst. The sun sets, a light breeze fills the air as the waves crash on the beach.

Unexpected twists

On arrival to the hospital, she receives the news that Michael is fine and only has a concussion, and will stay the night for observation. She walks into his ward and greets him with tears rolling down her face and a big smile, as the relief starts to set in. Sitting at this side, holding his hand tightly, tears still rolling down her face as she says, that she thought she might have lost him. He calms her with a wink and a smile, jokingly asking what their plans are for tonight. He proceeds to tell her about the accident, that another car crossed the intersection and they collided head on, his car was totalled and first responders to the scene were in complete disbelief that he didn't have a scratch on him as these type of accidents are usually fatal.

He eventually convinces Bianca to go home, after she refused to leave his side, as the reason he was on the road, was that he dropped something off at her place for her. After this incident, any and all doubts in her mind about their relationship and marriage has disappeared, and she decides to fully embrace and follow her heart. On arriving at home, she finds a box on her doorstep, inside a photo frame with a picture of her and Michael, a note read 'a moment made eternal' a bottle of wine, a note 'like a fine wine to the taste, is your smile to my soul' a key to his place, the note read 'you already own the keys to my heart, here is a key to my place', he also had a cd that read 'mixed tape' with all the greatest love songs from the 60s till now in the box and a hand written letter describing his feelings for her, his gratitude for the memories they have made so far and even wrote a sweet and cheesy poem about her. A Dolphin teddy with a note, as vast as the oceans for a dolphin, so is my love for you, and also cause you love dolphins so much!

Back at the hospital Michael learns the other driver from the accident is just down the hall, and decides to check on her. Lying in bed with a broken wrist, he meets Michelle who can't apologize enough for the accident. She has had so many problems with her car and didn't have the finances to get it fixed, the brakes failed and her car was also totalled. As with Michael the first responders also couldn't believe how lucky she was, telling her it's an absolute miracle. She then admits that she asked God, that if he does exist, if he does care about her to give her a miracle. Discouraged she said, this was not what she meant, she is a single mom, struggling to make ends meet, her 10 year old boy's father left when she was pregnant with him and she also has a 5 year old daughter, her husband left her for another woman. Deeply troubled by her circumstances, Michael feels compelled to help her, without knowing how, his car was insured, and hers was not. She was just thankful that her parents picked her kids up from school and that they were safe.

The next day on his release from hospital, Michael gets a visit from his cousin, Steven. Michael tells his cousin of his intention to marry Bianca, and to ask her in the coming weeks, not looking to waste more time, as he knowns beyond any doubt that she is the one. Steven is very happy for his cousin, but saddened within himself. He has always wanted a family of his own, but is unable to have children, already in his forties, he has everything to offer, even has a three bedroom house, and all the things money can buy, his dad even owns a wine estate outside Cape Town where he is an apprentice and will soon take over, but unable to have the things that really matters to him, the priceless things. He always ends up with gold diggers as he would describe them and never a real down to earth woman who loves him like Bianca loves Michael.

As Michael shares his experience he had the day before and Michelle's circumstances, Steven shakes his head, laughs at Michael and says, God has such a sense of humour. He tells Michael about a competition he entered at a local grocery store just for laughs, and he won a small, brand new hatchback! He collected the car yesterday, not knowing what to do with this little car, thinking of maybe selling it, or giving it to someone, and after hearing Michelle's story he decides to give Michelle the car. Too excited to wait, they arrange to meet Michelle at her place. Just to drop something off to help her recovery. Handing her the keys, she first refuses and eventually in disbelief and overwhelming gratitude accepts, in tears as the two guys try to keep their own tears back. She insists that Steven, Michael and Bianca come over on the weekend for dinner, just as a small thank you. Steven drops Michael off at home, awaiting him in is Bianca, saying that she is here to take care of him and wanted to make good use of her new key to his place.

At the dinner, new friendships are formed, and Steven would meet his future adopted children and have his first official date with his future wife, without realising it at the time.

Over the next several weeks, Michelle and Steven gets to know each other better, falls in love and becomes a beautiful couple, and eventually a beautiful family.

Michelle's accident, turned out to be a miracle beyond what she could imagine at the time, a prayer answered not how she wanted, but with more than she hoped for. She lost her broken car, but gained a brand new car, new friends and even the right man for her and a father for her two kids, while Steven would finally have the right woman in his life and the opportunity to be a dad. God can really use everything towards good, an unfortunate accident, revealed as destiny. Beauty from brokenness.

Michael and Bianca's latest video that reached a million views before it was removed from the platform, due to community standards, they discuss and warn people about artificial intelligence, AI, and how man has created his own god in his own image, an omnipresent, ever present, all knowing, never sleeping god, providing answers to any question, that monitors all data from all people, running all financial transactions, calculates threats and suggests solutions as a collective knowledge base of all humanity, working towards peace, safety and unity for all mankind. People rely on AI more every day and the religion of AI worship is the biggest growing religion in the world. AI can create anything from nothing in the digital world and controls everything online. Some people even use AI as a form of companionship.

They host their friends for a social. Being very informed on world events and how it relates to Biblical prophecy, they talk about the significance of the peace deal struck between Israel and Saudi Arabia a week ago as part of the Abraham accords, bringing peace across the Middle East. Neil scrolling on his phone, suddenly jumps up, runs to the TV and switches to the news.

In Breaking news, While many Jews were praying at the western wall, a terrorist organization launched a rocket at the people below, the weapon malfunctioned and the rocket has completely destroyed the dome of the rock on the temple mount, with fires still raging on the mount, absolute chaos all over the old city, the military has been deployed and the perpetrators arrested. The event has caused stronger alliances amongst all the nations that was once enemies of Israel, condemning the incident, as they unite against a common enemy.

Everyone is shocked as they are pined in front of the TV set, watching it unfold, knowing they are seeing something historic and significant playing out in front of them. Eventually everyone goes home, and continue living their lives, as this group has realised that you can't be too upset about events outside your control, and that you have to remain calm, focused on God and the path that you are on, and the things you can influence.

Bianca joins Jenni and Neil on an outreach program in the Northern Cape for two weeks, to serve the communities in the rural areas. The time she and Mike spends apart, creates a longing and a new appreciation for each other, knowing they are only four hours apart, yet it feels like they are separated by an ocean. They count the hours until they see each other again. The time apart did give Michael more time to work on a marketing proposal for his uncle's vineyard, and catch some extra time kite surfing with Steven. On Bianca's return, the two spend some quality time the weekend alone at home, as if they haven't seen each other in forever.

During the weekly meeting, the CEO announces that all employees will have to be microchipped, and that it will be mandatory. All major companies across the world has enrolled this, and it is both for security purposes as well as complying with international standards. It has already become the norm in China and across Europe, and gaining popularity in the States. Michael raises the concern that this is the mark of the beast and due to religious reasons he will not comply with this. He is met with laughter around the boardroom, and suggestions that he should start looking for a new job then. On sharing this news with Bianca, she applauds his stance and encourages him that God will make a way, and that He would open another door. This mark is accompanied with a vaccine that they claim boosts the immune system and prevents any and all sickness known to man, however the side effects has been censored, that include a drastic increase of heart attacks amongst the youth, infertility in more than half of woman and also an increase in mental health disorders and depression.

They view breaking news from Jerusalem as the man from Syria, who they call 'the Assyrian' who brokered the peace deal between Israel and Saudi Arabia, the same man who brought unity to religion through the Abrahamic Faith Movement, a man who is highly respected by world leaders and admired by nations, seen as a messiah by many, a man of peace and unity, a charismatic man of authority, has announced that the temple mount should be a place of worship for all nations, and that the third Jewish temple will be built were the dome stood, so also a church tower to the north of the mount for those more drawn to Christian side of the Abrahamic faith and the al Aksa mosque in the south. Jews see this man as Elijah or even the Messiah, Muslims as the Mahdi and many Christians compare him to Jesus of the modern world, but there are those who see him as the antichrist, and these people are labelled as 'extremists and divisive people against peace and unity'

As the winter draws to a close and it's the start of spring, it's Mike's birthday, and Bianca has made plans to make it his best birthday ever. She's baked the cake, served him breakfast, got two tickets to a concert of one of his favourite bands, a romantic night planned just for the two of them, then a boys day out of kite surfing and rugby, while she organises his surprise birthday party for the evening. At the party, Michael looks around the room filled with friends, family and his girlfriend, thinking back to his previous birthday at TGI's with Jason and Nicole back in Atlanta, where he was in life, and how much has happened and changed over the past year.

His uncle brought him a bottle of the best wine and brandy from the vineyard and asked him if there was any way he could twist his arm to come and work for him. They can really use his skills and expertise in marketing and would love him to join the family business. Intrigued, he sarcastically responds that it would depend on the benefits. His uncle offers matching his current pay check, flexible hours, partly remote and as family, shares in the vineyard. Not needing to think a second about it, he accepts. Bianca puts her hand on his chest 'told you' Donovan also asks Bianca if she didn't use to be an event coordinator, as he needs someone to assist from time to time. So as one door closes, another is opened, and a prayer is answered.

While world events keep getting stranger, It has been an interesting winter in the Cape of Good Hope for Bianca and Michael who found love, purpose, friendships and a new place to call home.

On a hill top

As autumn begins in the States, spring is in the air in the Cape of Good Hope. Michael and Bianca, falling more in love each day as their love keeps growing stronger, while Steven and Michelle has found a new love in each other, Neil and Jenni already matured in love and marriage. All find themselves in different seasons of love and the beauty that comes with it.

Michael has won a national award on a marketing campaign he implemented and executed successfully, as he resigns to start a new job at his uncle's vineyard, much to the disappointment of his boss. His book is still selling copies worldwide, and is very popular in India and Brazil. The channel he and Bianca runs is still influencing thousands as their social group keeps strengthening and expanding. Bianca is looking for a way to earn extra income and apply her creative side. As the weather becomes more favourable it presents new opportunities and possibilities.

It's a beautiful spring day in Cape Town, Bianca awakens to Michael sinning happy birthday while bringing her breakfast in bed, then kissing her forehead, her lips, down her neck, shoulder and her hand. He has the whole day planned out, the gift, the pick nick, Two Oceans Aquarium, sunset Champaign cruise and the evening dinner party at a nearby restaurant with their friends. She has a quick video call with her mom and sister, who she misses dearly, wishing her happy birthday. They also reveal their plans to visit her in the nearby future, a visit she awaits eagerly. After an eventful day filled with fun and romance, Bianca and Michael are the last two remaining at her party. Streamers and balloons all over the floor, sitting at the table having a glass of wine, Michael takes her by the hand and leads her to the dance floor, slow dancing to a song on his phone, lost in each other's eyes, just the two of them, putting an exclamation point on the best birthday she has ever had, with the best man she has ever known.

The following day, Bianca waiting excitedly for Michael to pick her up for some surprise, sees his car pull up on the driveway, and then the surprise, her mom and sister gets out of the car and the excitement of all three is clearly visible as they share a long tight hug. Michael has bought them plane tickets and arranged accommodation for them, as a part of Bianca's birthday present. The four spend the day together as the couple shows them around. Early the following morning they drive up the West coast for a couple of days break away, so that Bianca can spend some time with her family, and so Michael can get to know them better. They found a little piece of paradise here, a small town resembling the islands of Mykonos and Santorini, with Greek style architecture throughout the town, with a crystal clear lagoon and pure white sandy beaches. The usual dry and barren land has transformed into a Garden of Eden, with wildflowers blooming everywhere for miles upon miles. They turn off the main road onto a gravel road and drive a couple of miles, surrounded by flowers of every colour that you can think of, stretched out across the plains, valleys and hills. Arriving on a hill top, they decide to take a walk through the wildflowers, the sight can only be described as 'a garden of God' or a vision of heaven. Michael plucks the most beautiful flower he could find and gently puts it in Bianca's hair as Jackie captures the moment with a photo. The evening they enjoy the catch of the day with a glass of wine and spend the next couple of days exploring this beautiful place, together. One evening the two sisters go out for a girl's night, and Michael takes Bianca's mom, Sarah out for dinner to ask her a very important question, for her blessing to marry her daughter. She approves, saying they are perfect for each other, and she has never seen her daughter so happy. She loves this place on the west coast so much, she is considering moving here after she goes on pension.

After a few days in paradise, they return to Cape Town, and Michael gives Bianca some space to spend time with her sister and mom. He has booked a Spa day for the ladies, and after a relaxing day of treatments, Jackie hands Bianca a gift. On opening the gift, she finds a beautiful red dress, a dress she pointed out to Michael a couple of weeks ago, that she thought was too expensive. Jackie asks her to try it on. She looks phenomenal! Her mom then suggests that she shows them Signal hill, Bianca's favourite place and where she first fell for Michael, where they had their first amazing moment. They drive up the hill as the sun starts to set over the bay. Arriving at the top, Bianca is greeted by Jenni, handing her a bouquet of wild flowers and directing her up a path, aligned with candles. Looking back, her mom and sister holding hands, smiling with tears in their eyes, nods in excitement. Her heart starts to race as she walks up the path, as if floating and time appears to be standing still. Neil greets her and crowns her with a tiara. As she keeps walking up the candle lit path, the nervous excitement keeps mounting, Michelle hands her a note that read 'You were born for me, and I was made for you' followed by Steven handing her a note reading 'from the moment I met you, since before I knew you, till the end of the age and into eternity, my heart belongs to you' She finally reaches the top, candles and flowers everywhere, but no one there, just a note on the ground. She reads the note, 'at this very spot a couple of months ago, I met my soulmate, now it's time to fulfil destiny' Neil starts playing their song on his guitar, She hears Michaels voice calling her name, as she turned around, there he was on bended knee with a ring in his hand. Looking up at her, his eyes filled with tears of joy he asks her to marry him. Her hand covering her mouth, shaking and trembling with excitement and shock, she nods her head, and repeatedly says yes, louder and louder. He puts the ring on her shaking finger, passionately kisses her in an intimate embrace, while their friends and family cheering on and everyone tearing up. A moment written into eternity. They all celebrate the big moment with Champaign, hugs and high fives. Neil plays their favourite 80s love song on his guitar as the two slow dance in the moonlight, the city lights to the one side and the Atlantic to the other, up on a hill top.

In a loveless world, these two found true love, people have followed their desires and given themselves over to lust, while Michael and Bianca has given themselves over to God, followed their hearts and found love.

At the engagement party, Jackie and her mom are already discussing wedding ideas. What a beautiful night it was! Michael's uncle Donavan has a family wine estate, just an hour's drive from Cape Town, it has been in the family for generations and is also the place that Michael's dad grew up, before he left for the States. Dutch and French style architecture from the 18 hundreds, and a row of jacaranda and cherry blossoms trees welcomes you to the farm at the foot of the majestic Langeberg Mountains, called Becheur estate. A night of laughter, dancing, romance and delicious local cuisine, celebrating the lovely couple's engagement. His uncle has also offered to host their wedding for them, as an engagement present. The following morning the couple takes a hike up to the Yellowwood tree, a tree his great, great grandfather planted, and from there they have an amazing view of the farm, vineyards, the mountain range and Table Mountain in the distance. 'This is the place', whispers Bianca with her arms around his neck, staring into his eyes. 'This is where I am going to marry you.' He kisses her on her forehead and replies, 'it's perfect'

Later the day he drops her off at her place, and they discuss how difficult it always is to say goodbye, how they miss each other and how much it sucks to wake up alone. After all they are engaged, she already has a key to his place and they have a wedding venue, her mom and sister is still there, and they decide to get married the very next weekend.

Everyone chips in and helps to make the arrangements for the wedding as Bianca with her mom and sister goes dress shopping. The couple are not allowed to see each other till the wedding, as the whole week is spent in preparation for the big day. Michael's sister and brother in law will even be able to fly down for the wedding, and decide to make a holiday out of it.

Friday evening, and its only hours away and the longing and excitement Bianca and Michael has is consuming. Everything has been arranged and tomorrow is the big day. After Michael had a bachelor evening with the guys, he remains behind at the crackling fire, looking up at the stars as he takes a deep breath, realising that it is finally happening, filled with gratitude, he goes to bed alone, knowing it is for the last time.

Bianca is still up late, she and Jackie, as she can't contain her excitement and her nerves as she triple checks that everything is in order for tomorrow. In frustration she awaits the day to start, she keeps asking is it tomorrow yet?

The sun rises over the cape, and Bianca is up and acting like a child on Christmas morning, eager to get going. It's her wedding day! The ladies arrive at the venue and after brunch, it's time to prepare. Michael does final checks and confirmation that all is in place, his heart is racing, the nerves and excitement is overwhelming as he gets a quick haircut and gets dressed for his wedding.

It's late in the afternoon, on a hilltop, and under an yellowwood tree, a hand full of guests, a minister, Jackie as maid of honour, Steven as best man and at the end of a red carpet stands Michael, grey suit, black tie, struggling to stand still, as a horse carriage approaches, Neil steps down and helps Bianca step off the carriage, at this point Michael becomes relaxed and overjoyed, overwhelmed to see his bride approaching, with a sleek, elegant white wedding dress, with a slit up to her thigh, off the shoulder and backless, her beautifully styled brown hair and perfectly done makeup, she is absolutely radiant! She slowly walks down the aisle while not breaking eye contact with Michael as she has that extra sparkle in her eyes and a bigger than normal smile. Michael has tears of joy rolling down his cheek as he is completely focused on his bride, as time seems to be standing still.

Face to face the twos excitement and nerves are obvious, no words are spoken between them, and their eyes are completely fixed on each other. Like it was just the two of them, and nothing else and no one else was there. Michael left speechless on the appearance of his radiant bride, has forgotten his vows that he have been rehearsing repeatedly. He starts off, while trying to keep the tears back, 'I have never seen, nor do I have any words to describe the beauty that stands before me, I have no words to describe the love and gratitude I have for my bride, I can only thank God who blessed me so abundantly, and giving me this honour to love you with all that I am, forever. You are my dream come true, my heart, my life, my happiness, all that I am is yours. From the moment I met you, since before I knew you, till the end of the age and into eternity, my heart belongs to you. Both now tearing up, Bianca struggling to get the words out, You are my answered prayers, my dream come true, my God sent, my inspiration, my determination, my best friend, my safe place, my happy place, you are home. Everything I am, all I have to give, is yours! Everything has led me to you, and God will lead us forward, together from this moment into eternity.

After the normal I do's, they are pronounced husband and wife, he draws her close, they share a passionate, intimate kiss as their friends and family cheer them on. Photos are taken and the two proceed in the carriage to the reception as they can't keep their eyes or their hands off each other. An intimate and romantic wedding reception follows, music on an acoustic guitar, wild flowers and fairy lights, candle light and rose pedals. Slow dancing and beautiful speeches. They cut the cake and do all the normal traditions. The couple excused themselves and return to the honeymoon suite, where a long awaited unity from a passion and love that has been growing for months, a longing for each other is finally met. A moment of pure, intimate, spiritual, emotional and physical oneness as love overflows and consumes them to their most inner being. Everything that is unspeakable, indescribable through mere words are physically exclaimed. All senses are in hyper drive for each other and disabled to all its surroundings. They eventually pass out in each other's arms after being overwhelmed by each other. As the sun rises over a new day, they wake up in each other's arms, as husband and wife. After being together again, and enjoying a shower, they meet their friends and family for breakfast, where else but under an yellowwood tree on a hill top!

Michael's sister and brother in law are staying at his place for the week, while Bianca's sister and mother are returning back to the States. Bianca and Michael are off on honeymoon in the Drakensberg Mountains and Blyde Canyon for the week. An entire week of waterfalls, mountains, canyons, restaurants, sleeping in and half the time spent in bed.

They have become one, physically, emotionally and spiritually. One being, yet two people.

Once returning home, Bianca moves in and as the place was a bit of a man cave, they repaint the townhouse and Bianca decorates, to give it a female touch and make it homier. In the lounge they hang a big canvas of the photo Jackie took of them in the flower fields, and in the bedroom a canvas of their wedding day.

How wonderful it is, to fall asleep in each other's arms every night and wake up holding each other tight each morning. Doing absolutely everything together, the two is inseparable. Whether they are out and about, with friends, dressing up for events or binge watching series in sweatpants, making dinner and washing dishes, feeding the poor, assisting the old, entertaining and educating orphans, leading small groups, they carry and support each other. He is her strength, and she is his weakness. They have even started learning the local language -Afrikaans, and Michael also applied for citizenship by decent, for the possibility that they might want to stay here, permanently. It has been a spring like no other, an eventful and life changing season.

Summer of love

As December starts, Mike and Bianca go up to signal hill for the sunset, as they have started this tradition to celebrate the day they first met, every month.

Its summer time in the Cape of Good Hope, as tourists flock the region and there is always some festival or event happening. The weather is fine and the beaches are packed. Longer days and warmer nights presents so much more to do. While Mike and Steve kitesurf, the ladies take the time to get tanned, toes in the sand.

Sevens rugby festival, cricket matches, live music shows, theatre shows, beach activities, wine festivals, even a NBA Africa basketball game, all happening in the eventful December. The couple find it strange, yet exciting to experience summer in December, a Christmas in board shorts, a time for fun in the sun.

They still do their movie cuddle night, date night and romance by candle light, since the power is out nights. They have also discovered a new favourite thing to do, horseback riding at the family vineyard up to the yellowwood tree for a pick nick, and road tripping along the coast to visit lighthouses and small towns.

Michael is loving the new challenge of marketing and distribution at Becheur wines, and is looking to expand their brand in the States and increasing sales to Europe. In need of someone trustworthy and skilled he approached Jackie to be their representative and business development manager in the USA. She is absolutely thrilled, as she already has the contacts to make this happen, she can work from home and don't have to worry about getting that human branding microchip. Her mom is retiring at the end of the month, thinking of possibly taking her pension and moving to the Cape, where her money can go so much further, there on the west coast.

Bianca still busy with missionary work while she is planning an upcoming wedding on the Becheur estate, the harvest festival at the end of the summer. Mike and Sunshine, as he has nicknamed Bianca, join Steve and Michelle, on a double date for a theatre show, Dirty Dancing, based on a movie from the eighties and a dinner in Camps Bay. On the weekend they go on a road trip to Oudtshoorn via the breath taking Route 62, one of the most scenic routes in South Africa. The first night they camp under the stars next to a crackling fire before meeting up with Neil and Jenni the next morning to help with painting and renovations at a local church in Oudtshoorn. Late afternoon they prepare food for the orphans before hosting a youth evening. They end the evening around a born fire with Neil on his guitar.

Since the area is known for ostrich farming, they decide to visit a local attraction, where the guys participate in an ostrich race, until of course a crazy ostrich decided to charge Michael, who somehow manged to outrun the big bird, leaving Bianca laughing on the ground. On returning to Cape Town, they attend the all Africa NBA game, giving them something familiar from the states, even though they support opposing teams.

It's Christmas Eve on the Becheur estate. Christmas and fairy lights everywhere, with candles on the patio and a born fire in the yard. A Perfect Christmas table setting, with the head of the table left vacant, for the guest of honour Jesus as is tradition, around the table Michael, Bianca, Steven, Michelle, Jenni, Neil and their two kids, Donovan and his wife. Donovan welcomes everyone and opens with prayer, Neil does his Christmas bit on guitar and Michael makes a toast, 'to celebrate the birth of the saviour king, to the blessing of family we have here, the family beyond the sea, the friends that became family, and to the love of my life.' a Three course Christmas dinner, Cape salmon for starters, lamb roast, roast beef, gammon and veggies, followed by an English trifle for dessert. After dinner gifts are exchanged and a coffee is enjoyed at the born fire. Christmas morning Bianca awakens in Mike's arms and hints at coffee in bed, in the kitchen he finds another gift from Bianca, a big box full of chocolates, cookies and sweets from the States, each attached with a note describing the things she loves about him. He serves her coffee in bed and after breakfast the two head down to the animal shelter for their first stop of the day. They are there to drop of food, blankets and treats. As they unpack the goodies, Bianca finds a gift-wrapped box with her name on it, and on opening it finds a dog collar and leach. Asking excitedly what it is for, he replies, we're not only dropping things off, but picking someone up. He got her a sweet little 8 week old black Labrador, since they both love dogs and she hasn't had a pet in forever. With the lab, now named Coco in her lap they head to their second stop for the day, delivering presents and sweets to the orphanage and then prepare and serve a late Christmas lunch to people at the Soup kitchen. It has been a Christmas like no other before, as they arrive back home, physically exhausted, emotionally satisfied and spiritually filled.

A Week of relaxation and lazy summer days follow before New Year's Eve. Dinner, live music and dancing at a place called the Barnyard with their friends. Thinking back at how the year started, everything that has happened and where they find themselves now, is completely inexplicable and would not seem possible only twelve months ago. On the stroke of midnight, streamers and balloons fall from the ceiling, Champaign bottles are popped as they share a passionate new year's kiss, wishing each other a happy new year and thanking each other for the best year of their lives, knowing that even greater things are ahead. After an all-nighter they go up to signal hill to watch the sunrise on a new year, then a breakfast at the Green point lighthouse before picking Coco up at Neil and Jenni's.

The month of January were not short when it comes to world events, famine in China is gripping the nation, droughts in Europe and the middle east with rivers like the Euphrates, Danube and Rhine drying up and the biggest news, the Jewish temple construction that started on the temple mount. With wars between nations and civil wars, ironically the Middle East is one of the few places of peace and prosperity, along with this southern point of Africa.

Bianca is coordinating a wedding, and the guys are out for a day at the cricket, taking some boys from the orphanage with them. While having a blast, Mike gets a text from Home Affairs that notifies him that his application for citizenship has been approved. Bianca is excited and relieved of the news. They both decide to keep dual citizenship, as you never know what the future holds.

Towards the end of January its harvest time in the cape and the harvest festival at Becheur estate. The new marketing campaign Michael implemented along with the drought in Europe has increased export to record highs and Jackie has signed a big retailer in the USA to stock the wine as they expand their market in the States.

Harvest festival day has arrived, it's another beautiful summer's day in the Cape and the couples are all in competition, as they start by seeing who can harvest five baskets, destem and wash off the grapes the fastest, this is followed by grape treading to release the juices and start fermentation. Mike and Bianca has some fancy footwork, as they stomp, tread and dance on the crushing grapes. There is also a tour of the winery, horseback riding and then the release of the latest Chardonnay and Cabernet Sauvignon, a harvest from the previous year. Wine tasting is accompanied with various crackers, fine cheeses, fruits and nuts, Neil provides background music on his acoustic guitar, and in the evening, live music with dinner and dancing. After a successful Harvest festival, Mike helps cleaning up and congratulates his exhausted wife on the successful event. He draws a foam bath for her surrounded with rose pedals and gives her a massage. She falls asleep in his arms. On the way back to their place the next morning with Coco sleeping on the back seat, Bianca looks at some of the photos of them that they took the day before, a series of photos from the photo booth that she wants to develop into canvas prints for their place, to go with the portrait of them in the flower fields, of the picture her sister took. She scrolls through her phone, looking at all the photos and amazing memories they have made in only several months, never imagining she could be this happy and this lucky to have met the perfect guy for her. It's not his silver highlighted hair, his smile, broad shoulders or his romantic nature that she loves the most, but his imperfections, the way a strong man, can show her his weakness and be fragile with her. The way he walks with authority, yet cries while worshiping God.

Above their bed hangs a portrait of their wedding day, and in her closet is a shoebox full of memories, pictures and the little sentimental things she has saved. This beautiful place and this amazing love has reignited her love of photography and she starts to make a photo book to give to Michael for Valentine's Day.

Jackie, back in the States, has just started dating Kevin, a friend from school she has been growing close to. He is the opposite of the bad boy, player guys she is used to, but she is also happier than she has been in a long time. Kevin had a huge crush on her in high school, and she had a crush on him during college, but nothing ever came from it. They lost touch with each other, but randomly bumped into each over the years. They have had some vibes between them for months now and finally kissed for the first time on New Year's Eve.

For the first time in five years, Michael has someone on Valentine's Day and spending it with his wife, and Bianca is excited about the day for the first time in years, spending it with the love of her life, her husband. Bianca has made Michael a photo album of their memories made till now, and ironically Michael made her a video montage of their memories. Chocolates, massages, roses, gifts, cards, romance, the two try to out spoil the other with gifts and pampering. The next day, they receive news that Steven and Michelle got engaged and another wedding at Becheur estate is on the books!

Meanwhile Michael's book has been unpublished on all platforms on grounds of being against community and global standards. Christians have been officially deplatformed from all forms of media and the internet as a whole, the Bible itself has been combined with the Quran and edited to accommodate the Abrahamic faith. The One world government has now taken full control over nations, religion and financial systems. Properties are no longer owned but rented, as it has become too expensive to buy and banks are making more money while owning the assets, there are no more financing available, no more debt can be made, and no more money can be invested, it has all been centralised. Money has become digital and has an expiry date, ensuring the economy is continuously stimulated. Electric vehicles are only permitted to drive a certain range before they shut down, while the price of gas has surpassed $300 a barrel, mostly due to carbon tax, making it too expensive to drive long distances.

A Trip around the Sun

The pleasant warm summer days makes way for the cooler days of autumn in the Cape of Good Hope. Bianca's mom sold her house in the States and moved down to the west coast of South-Africa and bought a blue and white Greek style bed and breakfast overlooking the ocean. Michael and Bianca's calling has been completely shut down online and they have started investing more time and effort into their home church that has been growing and missionary work in the communities that has brought much change to people's lives. Living in love and living with purpose they have found abundance and prosperity against all odds and by the grace of God always stayed one step ahead and being able to avoid the draconian rule that surrounds them. Everything they do is successful and everyone they serve are blessed.

During the autumn months they have enjoyed each other, covered in love, their love has inspired others and restored broken relationships, and God has worked through them to bring many to the faith, while Becheur estate has seen its best two quarters in decades.

Steven and Michelle got married, also at the family vineyard where Michael and Bianca were best man and maid of honour in a beautiful autumn wedding. Coco is getting big and developing such personally and showing massive intelligence. Once a month the home church does an outreach day to the local shelter, while they are also involved in helping the community with food, shelter and orphans with food, toys and education.

Towards the end of autumn, international travel enforced digital passports to be microchip only as Bianca and Michael realised they would never be able to go back to the states or see his and her sister ever again. The place they have come to know as home, that they were renting also came with the news that it will receive the digital chip and renters would require the chip themselves as the new renter system has now reached the Cape. This left them with the only option to move to

Becheur estate and they realised that everything they have been spared from is now on their doorstep. Knowing as always though that God will provide and sensing that they will witness the end of the world. The only thing that kept them at peace till now has been them, focused on God and not the circumstances.

After spending their first seven months as a married couple in this home, they start packing with sadness and gratitude for what was, and what is still to come.

After the movers packed everything up, Michael lit a couple of candles, put on some music, ordered take out and gave Bianca one last memory of this place, before saying goodbye.

It has now been an entire year since Bianca and Michael arrived in the Cape, since the day they first met. To celebrate this, they are on signal hill at sunset as they reflect on all the things that has happened over the last year. They have dinner at the same restaurant and even spend the night at her former cottage, in Neil and Jenni's back yard. Michael gets the fire place going, it starts raining outside, and they spend the evening in each other's arms, knowing that everything is going to be alright, and in spite of what's happening in the world, they have had the best year of their lives.

Moving to Becheur estate, has turned out to again be a blessing, they have given up something great and familiar for something even greater. The place is bigger, they can walk to work, horseback riding and roaming all over the estate, with much more place for Coco to play. Getting back to nature and spending time with God and their loved ones. Luckily they have died for the things of this world, as all forms of travel, sport and entertainment requires people to have the digital mark. So many people were unwilling to give up the things of this world and complied. Many in poverty took the mark to receive their universal basic income, and others did so to have access to healthcare.

On a cold and rainy Sunday morning, Neil on his way to pick up supplies for the soup kitchen, is in a car accident on the freeway, he was declared dead on arrival at the hospital. After receiving the devastating news Bianca and Michael make their way to Jenni and the kids. Over the next few days they arrange the funeral, while staying with Jenni and her kids. More than a thousand people attended his funeral and testified to Neil being a man of God who left a big void behind, together with a legacy of how to serve God and love people.

Jenni decided to honour his memory by continuing the work that they have been doing and persist in what God has called them for. Michael and Bianca has also stepped up, by spending more time with the two kids.

Michael started having dreams on a regular basis, dreams that felt real, as if almost a memory, and always something spiritual. In one dream he was with Bianca and she had a baby with her, they were on the beach in the evening, when there was a loud trumpet blast, as loud as thunder, then the night sky became brighter than day light, almost blinding for a moment, followed by absolute silence, then the sky was torn open and it felt like he was being pulled out of his body. In another dream he was standing on a mountain with a great multitude with him, some was looking up at the sky with great sadness and despair, others were standing around looking down at their phones, when suddenly a meteor appeared in the sky, ripping through the atmosphere, louder than a low flying fighter jet, crossing the sky in seconds as night appeared as day light, an eerie silence was followed with an enormous earthquake that tore the mountain in two. The final dream he had, he saw the Ark of the Covenant being paraded through the streets of Jerusalem to the temple mount, it was placed before the temple, opened, and the ten commandment on stone tablets was revealed, then the ark was moved into the temple. Suddenly there was a throne at the entrance to the Holy Place, a man was sitting on the throne and the Pope placed a crown on his head, while ten presidents bowed before him.

He immediately understood exactly what these dreams meant, as one being the rapture, one a meteor hitting the earth and one the dedication of the temple and the antichrist's seat of power.

He shared these dreams with Bianca and their home church and several other men also shared similar dreams they've had over the last month of the rapture, the temple and the antichrist. Some even shared dreams where there were blackouts over all the earth, complete darkness for three days, day and night, with no stars visible in the sky, only a blood moon.

Bianca and Michaels love and affection for each other has increased even more, as they love each other as if there is no tomorrow, still filled with peace and joy, not fearful of anything that's happening but have a sense of urgency and their mortality, to truly make every day count.

The shortest and driest winter on record for the Cape has ended in two months as spring came earlier than ever before and record temperatures are predicted for the coming summer, also having an enormous effect on agriculture.

Over in the states, Jackie has been living with Kevin, struggling with her faith, but steadily growing, Michael's sister and brother in law has been fired from their jobs, for not complying to the national mandate on microchipping. They've taken their son out of school, and he is currently being home schooled. They have managed to buy six months' supply worth of food and are looking at what options they have available going forward.

Back in the Cape, Bianca has been nauseous the last couple of days and missed her time of the month. She took three pregnancy tests, as she and Mike, are sitting anxiously waiting for the results to appear with nervous excitement. Three times, it's positive! They both want this, they embrace each other, overjoyed and overwhelmed. After they celebrate, they make an appointment with Bianca's gynaecologist to confirm, before they share the news. Suddenly reality sinks in, yes they want this, but she can't go to the hospital to give birth, how can they bring a child into the world as it is now, and with what is to come? How can this be such a blessing for them while also being such a concern? A Few days later, they visit the Gynaecologist, who confirms that she is eight weeks pregnant. Overjoyed again and overcome with emotion they share the news with friends and family, who all share in their joy.

As the spring came early in the Cape, in Israel autumn is in the air. The third temple has officially been completed and the date for its official inauguration and first rituals will be during the feast of tabernacles in mid-October. They have also stunned the world with news regarding the Ark of the Covenant, it has been missing for more than two thousand years, it will be revealed during the inauguration of the temple, and it has been in their possession for over thirty years, after it was found in a underground cave system, north of the old city by a biblical archaeologist, where it was hidden for centuries.

Bianca's journal -It's been over a year since I was single sitting on Miami Beach, without the possibility of love, living in the USA, with financial prosperity and worldly pleasure, but without purpose. Now I'm married to the love of my life, calling the Cape my home, living in purpose, peace and joy. Happier than I ever thought I could be. Life is no longer happening to me, or with exhausting effort, for me, but now life is happening from me, by letting go and letting God, more than I prayed for is now my life. Speaking of life, I have new life growing inside of me, as we are pregnant! I'm filled with excitement and anxiety with the uncertainty that lies ahead, but so far it all seems to have worked out great to live in faith of the unseen. Life is unpredictable, your story can change completely within one year, in a season you can discover purpose, in a moment find love, in only a second lose a family member, and also gain a family member. I have been reminded how temporary everything is, that it comes to and end before you are ready to move on, but that things have to make way for better things. I guess my biggest lesson I learned over the past year is that I have no control, just like everyone else, on what is going to happen next, but just to trust that God already knows, I don't have to figure it out, I just have to hold on to him and live in the moment with gratitude and obedience. Every beginning has and end, and sometimes the end of one thing is the beginning of a new thing.

Spring blossoms

It's September and the start of the spring blossoms in the Cape, and autumn leaves in the northern hemisphere. After a difficult and trying winter, filled with challenges and twists, Michael sits next to Bianca on the couch gently rubbing her stomach, he's leaning towards a girl, and she is leaning towards a boy, but both just want a healthy baby. Michael already wants to start preparing and get ahead of things, while Bianca, just wants him to take it easy, its only 14 weeks. He has become over protective and even sweeter than usual. They decided on Oriana, if it's a girl, meaning 'a new beginning or new dawn' or Noah if it is a boy, meaning rest or comfort.

It's also that time of the year again, when the wild flowers on the west coast are in bloom. So the couple take a few days to visit Bianca's mom to just have fun and relax after a busy, eventful and emotional winter.

The flowers are in bloom, even more than the year before, all across the hills and valleys. They spend the entire day road tripping through fields of flowers and even stopped at the hill were they took their famous picture the year before to have a pick nick. On arrival at Bianca's moms place, they are greeted by her, and she shines different than usual. She has a happiness and a peace Bianca has never seen, suggesting that she might have met someone, and looks like she is in love. The bible lies open on the coffee table next to a notebook, filled with notes, quotations and references. A deeper gratitude and love for God, pension and the west coast has made her a new woman. She has made many friends in the short time she has been living here and frequently meet new people through the guest house. The couple enjoy sleeping in, strolling through flower fields, golden sunsets, walking hand in hand on sandy white beaches, swimming in the crystal clear lagoon and enjoying moms cooking and company.

Back home Michael gets a boma fire going, while Bianca prepares a snack platter for them. The two sitting by the fire, with Coco outstretched next to them, they both has this sense and anticipation of something coming and big changes, some of it is the baby, but most of it, is something else, that they sense and cannot explain.

The following weekend its Jenni's daughter, Chelsea's birthday party at Beucher estate, the first since Neil passed away, and they have pulled off all the stops to make it a big and memorable birthday for her. Jenni seems to be doing alright, she has peace, but you can see the sadness in her smile. A few minutes after blowing out the birthday candles, Chelsea walks excitedly up to Michael, telling him that she wished that Jesus would bring her dad to visit just for today, but Jesus said that he and her dad was preparing a surprise party for her and that she will see him very soon. With tears in his eyes he hugged her and replied, you will Chels, you will. Knowing it's only the words of a child, but also taking what she said serious, he shares this with Bianca and tells Chelsea to go tell her mom exactly what she told him. Michelle on hearing this shares her feeling that she's been sensing for a while now something is coming, something is about to happen and even Neil admits to having a sense of expectation.

Michelle, Steven and the kids are a beautiful, happy family and their kids are good friends with Jenni's kids. While the kids are playing, the ladies are hanging out on the patio and the guys are on grilling duty. Steven shares with Michael news coming from his contacts he has in government and with high profile clients from China. The Chinese has been buying up property and land just over the mountains in the Wellington and Ceres area, and over the next couple of months they are expecting twenty thousand Chinese citizens to arrive in South Africa. The reason for this, is that it is believed that the meteor that was confirmed that will pass the earth in the coming year, will in fact hit, and make impact in the South China Sea. This would wipe out a third of the world's population, from China, Japan, the Philippines, Korea, Indonesia, even as far as India. They discuss that this would fulfil the prophecy in revelation regarding the mountain that fell into the sea and killed a third of humanity and a third of ocean life, and that this would be a strong probability. The governments has kept this under wraps, to avoid panic, economic collapse and the inability to relocate almost 3 billion people in several months. All information regarding this has been censored, labelled disinformation, and some people have ended up in jail, disappeared or committed suicide. The expected immigrants are all delegates, high profile business men and scientists.

As the kids quite down and fall asleep while watching a movie, the couples are outside, having their own little party. Bianca and Mike suggest that they will take the kids next weekend, so that Jenni can have a couple of days break away to Bianca's mom's guest house, being a long weekend, a suggestion she happily agrees to with deep gratitude. Michael volunteers to take Michelle's kids also for the weekend, so they can have a couples break away.

So the following weekend Jenni heads to the west coast, Michelle and Steven are off to the garden route to the south, while Bianca and Mike will have their hands full with four kids back at the Beucher estate. Michael, super excited for the weekend decided they will all go camping up on the hill of the estate, fire with marshmallows, fire place stories, under the stars, a whole fun filled weekend outdoors. The kids had an absolute blast, and Bianca and Michael may have enjoyed the weekend even more than the kids.

Sunday evening Bianca has a video call with Jackie, who is seriously considering taking the microchip as she can't go anywhere anymore and hardly do anything at all. She finds it hard to accept that all the fun and pleasures of life is over for her, and that it feels to her as if she has stopped living and is just surviving and waiting on death, while everyone else is having the time of their lives. Bianca convinced her, not to give up eternity for a few good times, or to betray Jesus for the insignificant things of this world. That in spite of how difficult things are, to just hold on, keep her focus on Jesus and not be distracted by what's happening around her.

Jenni arrives to pick up the kids, rejuvenated and relaxed, with the kids wanting to spend another night, she agrees and joins them in the tent to camp there the night.

At the end of September, Bianca is starting to show, as the pregnancy is going well. It's Rosh Hashanah in Israel, that is the Jewish New Year, and they have the biggest festival is their history, as the inauguration of the temple are just weeks away. The festival will be celebrated for ten days, each day at sunset, a new day starts and rams horns are blown, announcing a new day and a call to repentance leading up to Yom Kippur, the feast of atonement and repentance. As Yom Kippur starts the final and longer blast on the ram's horn is made. Michael and Bianca are following these feasts as they have discovered so much prophecy regarding the feasts and not as Jewish feasts, but God's feasts. On the third day of Rosh Hashanah there was a revival as never seen before in Israel, as more than a hundred and forty thousand Jews became followers of Jesus, as the media struggles to keep the story under wraps.

Just two days later, the United Nations appointed the Syrian, the great peacemaker as he is also known as the new leader, the tenth secretary general, making him the most powerful man in the world, already loved, respected and admired by millions. The pope, also present at the general assembly, praises the appointment and announces the secretary general to be the saviour the world needed, while Islamic nations have celebrated his appointment, with many viewing him as their Mahdi. With this news dropping, Michael receives a message from his sister 'we thought we won't be seeing each other again, looks like we will be seeing each other real soon'

Saturday morning, early October. Over in Israel, Yom Kippur starts at sunset, for the rest of the world it's a normal Saturday. Bianca and Michael spends the morning at the orphanage as they regularly do, afterwards they have lunch in beautiful Camps Bay, they follow this with a trip up to their spot, signal hill and end the day down at blouberg beach, overlooking the Atlantic and table mountain as the sun starts to set. Coco is chasing seagulls, a light breeze fills the air, Bianca sitting between Michaels legs, as she leans back, she looks up at him and tells him how much she loves him, and he kisses her on her forehead and tells her the same. As they sit in silence watching the sun set over the horizon, listening to the waves breaking onto the shore, when suddenly a silence fills the sky, the wind dies down and a loud trumpet noise, as loud as thunder fills the air, even the earth is trembling. Bianca grabbing onto him tightly, nervously whispers 'baby', he takes hold of her, looking up an intense light appears in the sky, the light becomes blinding and consumes the entire sky, and it feels like someone is pulling them up. He barely blinked, when suddenly Table Mountain was gone, the ocean was like crystal and had no waves, the sky was filled with every colour imaginable and the sky was alive, you could hear the colours. They slowly stood up, amazed, shocked and confused. As they turned to each other, they both had an appearance of being in their twenties and were both clothed in pure white clothing, radiating light. They both realised, that what they just experienced was the rapture. To their surprise Coco came running towards them, wagging tail and playful. They saw other people on the beach walking towards them, also dressed in radiant white, and as they came closer, recognised them, and started to run towards them. Michael hugged his sister, brother in law and nephew, while Bianca grabbed hold of Jackie and her mom, as they hugged and shared tears of joy. Bianca looked over her sister's shoulder and saw her dad standing there, putting her hands over her mouth. Jackie turned around and when she saw her father, ran to him, hugged him tightly and told him that she was sorry, as he replied the same. Michael's sister with a shocked look on her face, pointed and told Michael, look! Up from the beach was standing side by side, their parents, looking like they did, the day they got married.

Donovan, Steven, Michelle and their two kids Colin and Casey were also there just a few feet away. Bianca held her stomach, the baby? An angel that appeared as a man, no physical form but just light told her that the baby is fine, and will be one of the first born in the millennial kingdom. She will give birth to a girl, without any labour pain. But now we must go.

They heard voices of a great multitude, and as they headed up from the beach, there were millions upon millions of people, all dressed in pure white, radiating light that filled the skies. In the distance was a throne, as big as a mountain, and pure light was radiating from it, far more intense than the combined light of the millions of people. This light was alive, the source of all light, it was pure energy, absolute power, and there was love and acceptance in its rays, the light radiating from their clothes was the light of the throne reflecting its own glory. The ancient of days, the creator of all, God himself!

As Bianca looked to the side, she saw Jenni with her head on Neil's shoulder, Chelsea in his arm with Brett by his side.

In front of the throne a man appeared coming from the throne, he had the same pure light radiating from him, and he was dressed in scarlet, and had a crown on his head. Although he was miles away, they could see him as if he was only a couple of yards away. His eyes shined with love, and he had a presence of holiness and authority. He had a scar on both of his palms. It was the king of kings, the word that became flesh, it was Jesus. He picked up a large scroll, and on the scroll was seven seals, and only he had the right, the power and authority to open them. All the people there started shouting 'worthy is the lamb' repeatedly. Then a moment of silence followed. Michael grabbed Bianca's hand tightly, they looked at each other and smiled. In front of the throne, stood Jesus, and he opened the first seal.